TOP DOG

By Marcia Thornton Jones and Debbie Dadey

Illustrated by Amy Wummer

Hyperion Books for Children
New York

To my critique group: Mary Jane Biskupic, Carmela Martino, Jill McNamara, Pat Wolff, Jill Barrie, Fran Sammis, and Cathy Schwieger
—D.D.

To my two "top cats," Coco-Mo and Calliope!
—M.T.J.

Printed in the United States of America
First Edition
1 3 5 7 9 10 8 6 4 2
Book design by Dawn Adelman
This book is set in 14-pt. Cheltenham.
ISBN 0-7868-1549-3
Visit www.barkleyschool.com

Contents

FAME AND FORTUNE

"Roll over," Fred said.

Every last dog, all twenty of us, rolled over in the dirt.

Just once, I would like to tell Fred to roll over, but it didn't work that way at Barkley's School for Dogs. Each morning, Fred led us through a practice session and rewarded us with treats. I'd much rather be at home, protecting my human's apartment. After all, I do consider myself to be a Wonder Dog. Jack, the Wonder Dog. But Maggie, my human, didn't notice my

Wonder Dog qualities. If she did, she wouldn't think I needed to go to Barkley's School for Dogs.

Let me tell you something right up front, sitting and rolling on the ground isn't any walk in the park. In fact, being a dog, I thought a walk in the park would be better any day.

Things turned a little more interesting when Fred suddenly stopped the lesson. A strange woman and man carrying clipboards came into the play yard. At first I thought they were burglars. I barked a warning, but Fred tapped me on the snout and said the one word every dog dreads, "No!"

He didn't say it nicely, either. Here I was doing my job, protecting him and all the other dogs at Barkley's. What did I get for my trouble? Ouch! Humans can be so confusing sometimes.

I didn't want to go to time-out, so I

stopped barking. A dog hates time-out more than going to the vet. There's nothing worse than not being with friends.

Fred walked right up to the strangers and shook hands. I guess Fred knew what he was doing. Besides, these strangers had lots of great smells on them. The lady smelled like ham. I practically licked her knees off until she screamed, "Somebody get this dog off me."

Yelling like that can hurt a dog's ears. It hurts a dog's heart, too. Nobody likes to be yelled at—especially when they're trying to be friendly. I slipped inside an orange tunnel before Fred could snap a leash on me and put me in time-out.

Fred called Sweetcakes over to him. "This is the dog I told you about," Fred told the ham lady. "Sweetcakes is a true champ. I've entered her in next week's Grand Agility Championship. I'm sure she'll win."

I knew about the agility competition. That's where dogs ran through obstacle courses, including tunnels like the one I was hiding in. Sweetcakes made sure every dog at Barkley's knew about those competitions. It was a Fido Fact that she had competed in dog shows and won ribbons—lots of ribbons. Those ribbons Fred hung on the wall in a glass case so no dog could reach them. I couldn't figure out what good ribbons were unless I could chew them.

The ham lady looked over at Sweetcakes. "Hmmm," she said as she jotted something down on her clipboard. "Let's see what this dog can do."

Sweetcakes held her head high and glared over her shoulder to make sure every other dog in the yard had heard. "Look at this," Sweetcakes bragged.

Sweetcakes's buddy, a bulldog named

Clyde, grinned and panted, "Look, look." Clyde is a dog of few words.

Sweetcakes took off through the yard. She ran through tunnels, sailed over a bar, and even balanced on a teeter-totter.

Of course, Sweetcakes had done the course lots of times. "Look at her show off," I told my pal Blondie.

"Sweetcakes is good and she knows it, Jack," Blondie said with a nod. "But she falls short in the looks department."

Blondie knew what she was talking about because she's the most beautiful poodle I've ever seen. She had hair so white and fluffy it could've been mistaken for a cloud.

"Sweetcakes needs to improve her fetching," my buddy Floyd said. Being a beagle, Floyd knew about fetching.

"Sweetcakes has fetched Jack a few times," a slow, lazy voice said.

Blondie giggled, and Floyd laughed so hard he spit out the ball he'd been chewing. I glared at the basset hound snuggling in a pile of rags. Woodrow might be a bit on the lazy side, but he was also the smartest hound at Barkley's. He was one of my best friends, so I didn't get too mad at him for making a little joke. After all, Sweetcakes had swung me around by her teeth once just to see how far she could sling me.

You've probably figured out that

Sweetcakes is no angel. She's the meanest Doberman pinscher this side of the Mississippi. She likes to fight, and has one chewed-up ear to prove it.

"What are those people doing at Barkley's?" I asked.

Woodrow answered in a lazy voice. "They need a Top Dog for their commercial. The winner gets a lifetime supply of Top Dog Tidbits."

"Fang-tastic!" Floyd yipped. "That's dog-awesome!"

My mouth instantly started watering. I'd seen commercials for Top Dog Tidbits, and they looked like something I could really sink my teeth into.

Blondie hopped with excitement. "Commercials on television?" she asked, batting her eyelashes.

My eyes got fuzzy as I imagined myself as a television star. In my mind I could see ribbons draped from my collar and cameras flashing all around me. Fame and fortune would be mine. I'd even be allowed to chew on my ribbons. If I were the Top Dog, my human Maggie would see my Wonder Dog qualities.

"How do you know all this, Woodrow?" Floyd asked, interrupting my doggy dream.

Woodrow lifted one long ear. "These ears aren't just for looks," he said before turning around to nap. "They can pick up on a conversation a mile away."

It won't take them long to figure out the best dog for the job," I told my pals. I stood up extra tall, holding my shaggy tail as straight as a flagpole. I knew I'd make a great Top Dog. "Right guys? Blondie? Floyd?" I looked behind me. I had been deserted. My friends were already lining up in front of the TV producers.

2

TOP DOG

Blondie and Floyd pranced past the Top Dog visitors. As soon as Sweetcakes finished jumping over the last bar, Blondie almost tackled Floyd to be next to run the obstacle course.

Fred didn't notice Blondie and Floyd. Fred rubbed Sweetcakes's ragged ear. "I told you I had the best dog in the city," he told the visitors. "This baby has won so many ribbons I ran out of room to hang them."

The ham lady didn't look convinced.

"So you say," she said. "Let's see what some of these other dogs can do."

Blondie lifted her paws high as she made her way through the tunnel. I looked away when Blondie knocked down two bars from a jump.

Floyd went next. He made it through the obstacle course without dropping his tennis ball a single time. I could tell he was proud by the way he grinned with one lip curled up over his pointy teeth.

Woodrow walked up to the jump and sniffed as soon as Floyd was finished. Woodrow isn't what you'd call a fast dog. Woodrow sighed and headed back to his comfy pile of rags for a nap. "Don't feel much like jumping through hoops for anybody today," he told me.

"Don't you want to be famous like the rest of the dogs?" I asked him. "You'd get a lifetime supply of Top Dog Tidbits."

Woodrow shook his head, his long ears

sweeping the ground. "Fame isn't all it's cracked up to be," he said before settling back down for another nap.

Maybe fame wasn't for Woodrow, but I knew it was just the thing for me. But I didn't get to try out next because Clyde waddled to the front of the line. I didn't have to worry about Clyde. Jumping the bars with his stubby legs was almost impossible. Then he slipped on the teeter-totter and banged his nose on the ground.

Several other pups lined up to give the obstacle course a try. A white Westie chased a bird instead of finishing the obstacle course. Bubba, a black Labrador puppy, tried to wiggle his fat rump onto the teeter-totter without any luck. And a pug-nosed terrier kept sniffing the ham lady's feet instead of going through the tunnels.

The ham lady jotted notes about every dog on her clipboard. "What about him?" she asked, pointing straight at me. It had taken her long enough, but I was happy to see she finally noticed me.

Fred had been teaching us the agility course ever since I arrived at Barkley's. To me they were fun toys, but Fred had strange ideas about the jumps, tunnels, and teeter-totter that filled the backyard at Barkley's.

Fred sighed and looked at me. "Come here, Jack," he said. "Heel." Fred has this thing about the backs of his feet. "Heel," he said again. I ran to his foot and licked the back of his ankle.

"Cut that out." Fred held my ears in his hands and leaned down close to my nose. "Try your best," he said.

He had no need to fear. He was talking to Jack, the Wonder Dog. Before he even said, "Go!" I ran. I darted back and forth across the yard. I sailed over the tunnels and crawled under the bars. After all, that seemed to be the quickest way around them. Maggie would be proud of how fast I dashed around Barkley's yard. I galloped to the strangers and hopped up, poking their stomachs with my paws. That was a sure attention-getter.

Fred grabbed me and muttered something about practice making perfect. I figured that meant I was perfect. I held my tail straight and puffed out my chest. I was sure that I was going to be the new

Top Dog. Maggie would be the proudest kid in the city. That's why a flea could've knocked me over when the ham lady pointed at Sweetcakes.

"She's the one," the lady said. "Sweetcakes is our new Top Dog."

SOMETHING ROTTEN

Obviously, this human's brain was the size of a hairball. Sure, Sweetcakes had actually been to dog shows. I admit she's won a few ribbons, but that didn't make her a Top Dog.

"Now the whole world will know how great I am," Sweetcakes bragged. "You hounds stand back and watch a pro at work." Sweetcakes pranced around the yard like she'd won the ham bone prize of the year.

I shook my head. Couldn't these

humans see my Wonder Dog status? Didn't they notice my speed and my brains? My Wonder Dog looks? I pushed between Sweetcakes and the visitors, strutting my stuff just in case they hadn't noticed my full handsome coat, keen brown eyes, and my extra-large black nose.

"Get this dog out of here," the ham lady said. "We need to find a few extras for the commercial. This dog's in our way."

Her words hurt me down to the tip of my tail. After all, I am a Wonder Dog. Let me tell you, I am no ordinary dog. That's exactly what I said to my pals Blondie and Floyd.

Blondie looked away from me.

Fred scratched one of his floppy beagle ears and dropped his tennis ball. "No offense, pal," he said, "maybe this job isn't for you."

Blondie batted her eyelashes. "This

isn't just any job," she said. "These people can make a dog famous." Blondie batted her eyelashes one last time before turning her tail to me and trotting back to the ham lady.

"She has a point," Floyd said. He picked up his tennis ball and loped over to join Blondie around the Top Dog people.

My mouth watered again. We'd been working all morning and I was hungry. The thought of biting into a flavorful

tidbit made my stomach rumble. I'd never actually eaten one, but I'd seen the ads on television. Every time I saw one, I barked and barked, trying to get Maggie's attention.

Barking. It's a dog's way of talking. That's what I needed to do now. I needed to tell these television people they were overlooking the perfect dog for the job. "I could do it," I barked. "I was made for this job."

Nobody paid any attention to me. Every dog in the joint was wiggling and wagging their way around the visitors. Every dog, that is, except Woodrow and me.

Woodrow arose from his favorite napping spot and waddled over to me. "Forget about TV," he said with a kind voice. Then he raised his huge black nose and sniffed. "Something smells rotten about this whole deal."

Something was rotten, all right. Sweetcakes was the center of attention. I had to come up with a plan to prove to Maggie and everyone at Barkley's that I was Jack, the Top Dog.

4

MONSTER

The next morning, Maggie and I headed to school. I pulled her down the steps and weaved through all the people on the sidewalk. I dragged my favorite napping blanket in my mouth.

I had a great plan and I couldn't wait to put it into action. Was it my fault if my blanket tripped someone? Unfortunately, it wasn't just anybody. It was Miss Frimple.

Miss Frimple lived across the hall from us, and it was a Fido Fact that she didn't like dogs. She liked cats, instead. Today, Miss Frimple carried her cat, Razzmatazz; Tazz for short. Tazz and I were no strangers to adventures. Actually, I'd saved Tazz's furry behind more than once.

"Look what your dog did," Miss Frimple yelled as she scrambled up from the sidewalk. "He is a threat to all of humankind."

That was not true. I wouldn't hurt a

hair on Maggie's head—or Miss Frimple's, for that matter. I expected Maggie to tell Miss Frimple, but Maggie didn't get a chance.

Miss Frimple pointed across the street. "If you have to have one of those canine beasts, why can't you get a good one? Like that dog."

We looked to the other side of the street. A lady dressed in black walked a dog on a short leash. This was not your run-of-the-mill pound puppy. This black Lab's hair shone like it had been brushed three thousand times. With head high, it lifted its feet as though it marched in a parade.

The lady walking the dog looked very familiar. I held my nose high in the air and sniffed. Ham. Suddenly, it hit me. It was the ham lady! Had she found another Top Dog?

"What's with the rag?" Tazz asked me in

animal talk, making me forget all about the black Lab. Tazz squirmed to get down, but Miss Frimple held on tight. I had to feel sorry for Tazz, even if she was a cat. Being squeezed in Miss Frimple's arms must have felt like being stuck in Sweetcakes's jaws.

I dropped my favorite blanket to the ground. "I have a plan," I told Tazz. "I'm going to prove to everybody that I am Top Dog at Barkley's." I couldn't help but brag a little. After all, it was a brilliant plan.

Tazz looked at the blanket and hissed. "That thing looks like a flea's nest. Besides," she said with a bored voice, "being Top Dog is certainly nothing to brag about. In fact, being any kind of dog is nothing to brag about."

Tazz had a way of making the hair on my back stiffen, and a growl escaped my throat.

"Get that monster away from my cat," Miss Frimple snapped, lifting Tazz high in the air. She didn't need to bother. The last thing I wanted was a mouthful of cat hair.

SUPER DOG

"Never fear, Super Dog is here!" I barked as soon as Maggie dropped me off at Barkley's. I burst into the play yard with my favorite blanket firmly tucked in my collar to make a cape. A Chihuahua darted between my legs so fast that I almost tripped. Bubba, the puppy, tried to grab the blanket from my back. Luckily he slipped, or I might have lost my cape.

Floyd and Blondie trotted over to me. Blondie looked whiter than usual, her hair floating like a halo.

Floyd must've lost his tennis ball because he carried a leather camera case instead. I hated to admit it, but that camera case looked pretty good. Nothing makes a dog feel better than to chew on something, and soft leather was one of the best things to sink a dog's teeth into. "What's going on?" I asked.

Floyd dropped the camera case and grinned his lopsided smile. "Everybody's getting ready for the commercial," he said.

Blondie batted her eyelashes. "Fred gave me a bath and brushed me until my skin tingled." She did look beautiful. Of course, Blondie always looked good.

"This commercial is big stuff," she said. "I heard Sweetcakes might become so famous she'll leave Barkley's to be a Hollywood star!"

"Isn't that dog-awesome?" Floyd yelped. "We're hoping they will see us and put us in the movies, too. You better hurry or you'll miss out on all the action." Floyd and Blondie galloped across the yard to the cameras.

"Wait," I said, but it was too late. They were gone. Neither one had said a single word about my Super Dog cape.

I didn't like the idea of Sweetcakes being a Hollywood star one bit. On the other hand, if it meant she would leave Barkley's for good, then maybe it wasn't so bad. But if it was a movie star they were looking for, then they were looking in the wrong place. I had star quality. I had to make them understand.

I raced across the play yard so fast I'm sure my cape streamed behind me in a blur. I bet I looked like a super hero on TV. I hopped up on a tunnel and stuck out my chest. Lifting my nose to the sky, I howled. "It's Jack, the Wonder Dog to the rescue! I'm able to leap tall walls with a single bound and boldly go where no dog has ever gone before."

I took a deep breath and leaped into the air. For one brief moment I had the feeling of flying—of soaring. I felt like a bird. And then, I landed. Hard. *Splat!*

I lay on the ground for at least five minutes, waiting for the ambulance to come. Did it come? No. Did anyone come? No! I felt invisible. All the other dogs were busy getting their coats brushed and

fluffed. The whole yard smelled like a perfume factory. Was every dog in the commercial except me?

I limped over and plopped down in my favorite spot by the food bowls. I was disgusted, but at least I had my favorite blanket to curl up in. Everybody was so wrapped up with the television commercial, they didn't have time for me anymore. I had to do something, but what?

I grinned. I knew what got me lots of attention from my owner Maggie. I scratched the ground and wiggled my tail end to get ready. Then I let loose with a howl that would make a pack of wolves proud.

"HOOOOWWWWL!" I looked around. Nothing. I gave it another shot, this time a bit longer and a little louder. "HOOOOOOOWWWWWLL!" Nothing! I couldn't understand it; my howls had always gotten results before.

I scratched my chin and wiggled my tail end again. This time I would give it everything I had. "HHHOOOOOWWWLLL!" I got results all right. Oh boy, did I get results. The back door flew open and out stomped Fred. He carried a brush in one hand, and a can of hair spray stuck out of his pocket.

"What has gotten into you?" he asked as he grasped my collar. "Has all this commotion upset you? Maybe a nice quiet time-out is what you need."

Time-out! That was the last thing I wanted. I tried to wiggle away but Fred snapped a leash on my collar quicker than I could scratch a flea. He pulled me around the shed and snapped the leash to a hook.

"Jack, you have to be quiet. This is a big day for Barkley's and for Sweetcakes. I know you don't want to mess this up," he said before leaving me alone.

"Hey, big boy," a silky voice said from the top of the tall brick wall. "How come you always end up in trouble?" I looked up into Tazz's yellow cat eyes. She licked a paw and sneered at me. She liked to pretend she was smarter than me, but I knew better.

Tazz must have read my mind because she said, "If you're so smart, then how come I'm free and you're tied to a leash?" I didn't exactly know how to answer that, so I just kept my mouth shut.

"What's with the red cape?" Tazz asked.

"I was trying to liven things up," I explained. It wasn't the exact truth, but Tazz didn't need to know that.

Tazz stood up and stretched. "A yard full of dogs is bound to be a bit boring. Maybe I could make things a bit more interesting," she said.

"I wouldn't recommend it," I said. "Look where it got me."

Tazz licked one paw and then used it to

smooth her long whiskers, "You just don't know the right way to go about it. It's all about timing. I should know. I'm an expert at getting attention." And then Tazz jumped off the wall and disappeared.

SWEETCAKES, THE BABY DOLL

I wondered what Tazz had in mind, but it didn't matter because Fred came around the shed. He knelt down in front of my nose.

"Look, Jack," Fred said, "I'm sorry I snapped at you, but this is an important day for Sweetcakes. If things work out, then it's off to Hollywood for a whole series of commercials. You need to behave."

My heart felt like it was being squeezed. I knew how to behave. In fact, I could be better than Sweetcakes any day. Fred unhooked my leash and scratched my ears. "Come on, let's go watch the action," Fred said.

I bounded ahead of Fred and darted around the shed. Cameras pointed straight at a stage that had been set up under one of the maple trees in the yard. The Westie and two Irish setters sat on the stage. Clyde perched on a stool. Even Woodrow was propped in the corner of

the set. But none of that tickled the fur on my funny bone.

In the middle of the stage sat Sweetcakes wearing a huge pink satin ribbon and a baby's bonnet. I laughed. I couldn't help it. "Sweetcakes, the baby doll," I said with a chuckle. Sweetcakes looked in my direction and snarled, showing a yellow fang. Fred hurried up on the stage, trying to calm her down.

Blondie and Floyd saw me and loped

across the yard. A wad of paper was clamped between Floyd's teeth. "What happened to your camera case?" I asked.

Floyd dropped the paper at my feet and scratched under his chin before answering. "That lady isn't so nice when she catches you chewing on her things," Floyd said, nodding toward the ham lady.

"There's something about her that makes my fleas nervous," I said slowly, remembering how she strutted down the street with the shiny black Lab that very morning.

"Hhhmmmph," Blondie muttered. "She obviously doesn't know class when she sees it." She kicked at Floyd's paper with a slender white paw.

"I'm sorry you weren't picked for the commercial," I told her. I meant it, too. Blondie deserved to be in the commercial more than Sweetcakes.

"I just don't understand why they

chose that brute," Blondie said with a little whimper. I looked down at my paws, not wanting to see the hurt look in Blondie's beautiful brown eyes. And that's when my Wonder Dog eyeballs saw Floyd's paper for the first time. I mean *really* saw it.

OUT OF THE WAY

"Where did you get this?" I asked Floyd.

Sometimes Floyd picked up things he wasn't supposed to. He put his head down and tried to hide behind a floppy ear.

"Tell me," I said.

"We won't tell on you," Blondie added.

Floyd peeked out from behind his ear. "From her," he said, nodding toward the ham lady. "When she took the camera case away, I saw this paper sticking out of her pocket. I thought it might be tasty."

"What does it say?" Blondie asked.

"I'm not sure," I admitted. As many times as I'd seen my human Maggie reading her homework, I'd never figured out how she did it. Only one dog I knew might be able to read it. "We need Woodrow's help," I said.

We looked at the stage. Woodrow sat there, looking bored. I woofed and stomped my left paw in the dust.

Woodrow perked up one droopy ear and looked at us. "Woodrow, we need you!" I whined. Woodrow sighed and stood up.

"Cut!" the cameraman yelled.

"What's with the hound dog?" the ham lady snapped. "We're trying to make a commercial here."

Sweetcakes lunged at Woodrow. Fred grabbed Sweetcakes before she had a chance to land on Woodrow. "Maybe we need a break," Fred said. Fred may be a human, but he understood dogs.

Woodrow didn't seem to notice any of the hoopla. "What do you want?" he asked me as he hopped off the stage.

I motioned him behind a bush, away from the bright lights. Blondie and Floyd crowded near. "We found this," I told Woodrow. "Can you read it?"

Woodrow nosed the paper and cocked one eyebrow.

"What does it say?" Blondie asked.

"Tell us," Floyd demanded, wanting to chomp his teeth on the paper again.

"Can you read it?" I asked.

Woodrow looked at each of us before answering. "Of course I can read," he said.

"This is an advertisement for a dog show. The Grand Agility Championship."

"That's Sweetcakes's show," Blondie said.

Floyd nodded. "Sweetcakes has been bragging about it, but why would the ham lady be carrying this in her pocket?"

"Maybe the ham lady wants to enter her black Lab in the dog show," I said. My three friends looked at me like I had just sprouted a horse's tail.

"What black Lab?" Floyd asked.

"What dog are you talking about?" Blondie asked. I told my friends about seeing the ham lady with the black Lab.

"If Sweetcakes is doing commercials,

she wouldn't be able to go to that dog show, would she?" Woodrow said, his droopy ears sweeping the ground.

I looked at Woodrow for a full twenty-seven seconds before it hit me. "And with Sweetcakes out of the way," I said, "the ham lady's dog would win the contest!"

8

DEAD FiSH

"All right, roll 'em," a voice yelled from behind me. Naturally, my curiosity was aroused. You know the old saying, "curiosity killed the cat"? Well, I'm here to tell you curiosity is not so good for dogs, either. I couldn't help myself; I had to find out what was going on.

The television crew huddled around Sweetcakes and the other dogs on the stage. Naturally, I was worried for the strangers. Sweetcakes wasn't the kind of dog to put up with too much nonsense.

What was worse, now they were trying to make her eat when she clearly did not want to. "Come on, Sweetcakes," the ham lady said. "Eat just a little."

That proved they had picked the wrong pup to be in their commercial. I would've gobbled up that bowl of Top Dog Tidbits so fast it would've been a blur on the television. Not Sweetcakes. She sniffed the bowl, curled her lips over a fang, and growled.

"Come on, sweetie pie," the man said. "Eat. It's good." I sniffed. I could smell the Tidbits from across the yard. They smelled like dead fish. Obviously, Sweetcakes didn't like dead fish. She also didn't like to be called sweetie pie. Sweetcakes backed away from the bowl and growled again.

I watched the strangers try to get Sweetcakes to eat. Lights from four different cameras glared down on her.

Those strangers tried everything. The man even tried eating the snacks himself. That made my mouth water, but it didn't budge Sweetcakes. "Cut!" the ham lady finally yelled.

Fred hurried onto the stage and tried to fluff up the bow around Sweetcakes's throat. "What's the matter, Sweetcakes?" he asked. "Are you having a bad day?" Sweetcakes had a bad day every day, if you asked me. But I knew there was more to the problem.

"Take five," the ham lady called. Then she looked at Fred. "You have five minutes to get that dog in Top Dog shape." As Fred and the lady talked, I sneaked on the stage followed by my buddies.

"What's the problem?" I asked Sweetcakes.

"I hate this bow. I hate this bonnet. And I hate Top Dog Tidbits." Sweetcakes growled.

"But this is your chance to be a star," Blondie said from behind me.

"I don't want to be a television star," Sweetcakes snapped. "Sitting here dressed up like a doll is not my idea of a good time. I'd much rather be out in the yard where I can run and jump."

I could understand that.

"You mean," Woodrow said, "you'd rather be practicing for that show next week?"

Sweetcakes smiled. "I'm going to kick some tail at that dog show next week," she said. "I can't wait!"

DOGGY HAVEN

"Did you hear that?" I said. We huddled next to the brick wall, out of hearing distance. "Sweetcakes really wants to be in that show."

"She won't get to strut her stuff at the agility contest," Blondie said. "Not as long as she's Top Dog."

Woodrow looked up at the stage. Fred had just bit into a Tidbit, trying to prove to Sweetcakes how good they were. "Sweetcakes will be miserable as a television star," Woodrow said.

I looked at Sweetcakes. Her bonnet was lopsided and the big bow drooped below her chin. Sweetcakes had made my days at Barkley's a doggy nightmare. Did I really care if she was miserable?

"If she's in Hollywood, at least she'll be out of our hair," Floyd pointed out.

"But she'll be unhappy," Woodrow said.

I sat down to scratch under my collar

as I listened to my pals. It was true that without Sweetcakes Barkley's School for Dogs would be a doggy haven. No more growling. No more slinging me around. No more being scared.

Then I imagined Sweetcakes dressed like a doll and sitting still for hours while bright lights shone and cameras rolled. Sweetcakes was definitely not a sitting-still type of dog.

I knew, all the way down to the tip of my tail, that Woodrow was right. "Sweetcakes needs our help," I blurted, "or she'll be trapped in Hollywood and won't be able to win the dog show. We can't let that happen."

"Well," a bored voice said, "if you're going to do something, you better hurry."

We all looked up. There, perched on the wall was Tazz, swinging her bushy tail back and forth.

"Cathw!" Floyd nearly choked on the

paper he had stuffed in his mouth. I
nosed Floyd back from the wall.

"That isn't an ordinary cat. It's Tazz."

"Of course I'm not ordinary," Tazz
purred. "I'm extraordinary. But that's
beside the point. If you plan to stop the
commercial, this is the time."

We looked at the stage. Sweetcakes had
just taken her first bite of Top Dog Tidbits
and the cameras were humming.

10

YESTERDAY'S KiBBLE

"For whiskers' sake," Tazz said with a bored meow. "Remember what I told you earlier? It's all a matter of timing!" With that, Tazz hopped off the wall and landed right in Barkley's yard.

"What are you doing?" Blondie yelped.

"You're yesterday's kibble if Sweetcakes sees you," Floyd said.

Tazz rubbed her whiskers with a delicate paw. "I see that doggy brain of yours is working overtime, Floyd."

Woodrow grinned. "Tazz, you are a genius," he said.

Tazz took a moment to swish her tail. "Of course I am," she said. "Now, let's get busy."

"Allow me," Woodrow said with a wink. Then he raised his head and howled. "CAAAAAAATTTTTT!"

I had never heard Woodrow raise his voice. I didn't think he had the energy. I was wrong. Twenty dogs' ears perked in our direction; including Sweetcakes's.

One look at Tazz's bushy tail sashaying

across the yard was all it took.
Sweetcakes leaped off the stage, bonnet
and all, and raced straight for Tazz.

"Run, run, run!" I barked.

"My pleasure," Tazz said with a smirk.
Tazz dug her claws into the dirt and sped
across the yard, Sweetcakes close on her
tail.

Clyde waddled behind Sweetcakes as
fast as he could. "Cat. Get cat," Clyde
mumbled.

Bubba, the puppy, saw the commotion and galloped after them all.

Sweetcakes was fast, but Tazz was faster. She was also smaller. Tazz darted between people's legs and jumped over the cords connected to television lights.

Sweetcakes tried to follow. Only, Sweetcakes knocked over a camera. Clyde fell on Bubba and they both got tangled in the cords. Three lights crashed to the ground.

"Gct that dog!" the ham lady hollered.

"Get that cat!" Fred yelled. Tazz jumped over a camera and landed on the stage, right in front of the Top Dog Tidbits.

Things were definitely out of control. This situation was serious. Obviously, it was time for Jack, the Wonder Dog. "Out of my way," I barked. "It's Wonder Dog to the rescue!"

11

THE RESCUE

Okay, maybe it wasn't the smartest idea, but it was the only thing I could think of. I went over to the huge power plug that the cameras and lights were connected to and tugged. All the cameras went dead and so did the lights. Shadows fell over the yard. Everyone froze. Even Sweetcakes skidded to a stop and turned around to find out what was wrong. That was when Fred saw me with the plug dangling from my mouth.

"Get that dog!" the television lady yelled.

I wasn't going to let them get me without a fight. I zoomed across the backyard faster than a rabbit on a football field. I dodged people, jumped over dogs, and wove through all the commercial equipment. Cameras and lights toppled to the ground with loud crashes. That made me run faster.

I knew one thing for sure, if Fred got me I'd be back in time-out forever. But I had one thing on my side. Friends.

"This way," Blondie yelled. She nodded toward an empty tunnel. I ran in, then she and Floyd plopped in front of it. They acted innocent, but the lady was on to them. I heard her stomp across the yard. Two feet planted themselves in front of my buddies.

"Move, dogs," she snapped. "I have a commercial to make." She nudged Floyd out of the way and reached her hand into the tunnel. Her hand wasn't empty. It was full of Top Dog Tidbits. They smelled good.

I opened my mouth and did what came natural.

Don't worry, I didn't bite her. I gobbled up every Top Dog Tidbit she had. I had to crawl out of the tunnel to do it. Then I gave the lady a nice lick. I think she liked it. She smiled and rubbed my ear.

"Nice pooch," she said. "You're much nicer than that other dog."

I licked her again. I had to. Finally, a

human that saw Sweetcakes for what she was. Mean.

"Sweetcakes proved she doesn't have what it takes to be Top Dog—or a dog show champion," the lady said with a big grin. "Instead of Sweetcakes, I'm going to make you a star."

My ears perked up. Me? A star? "Did you hear that?" I asked Blondie and Floyd. "I'm going to be a star!"

Blondie frowned and Floyd looked at the ground. "What's wrong?" I asked. "Aren't you happy for me?"

Blondie sniffed. "Well, I am happy for you. But I had so hoped to be the star. After all, I just had a bath. You look like you haven't had one in a month."

I bristled. I'd had a bath just two weeks ago. Floyd scratched his ear and a tennis ball dropped out of his mouth. "I could be a star, too, you know," he said.

Now, I got it. They wanted to be the

stars. They were mad at me for wanting it too. I didn't want my buddies mad at me, but then I remembered Maggie. If I was Top Dog, she would see all my Wonder Dog qualities. My friends would have to get over it.

The lady led me back toward the cameras, but not before Sweetcakes walked up beside me. "You get in my commercial," she growled, "and I'll make you sorry you ever stepped foot inside

71

Barkley's School." Sweetcakes might not want to be a star, but she didn't want me to be one, either.

Clyde nodded. "Sorry. Yeah. Real sorry," he added.

I wasn't going to let any dog scare me out of my big chance to prove to Maggie that I was a star. I was going to do it, no matter what.

Just then, Woodrow waddled over to me. "Remember, fame isn't all it's cracked up to be," he said.

As usual, Woodrow was right.

12

THE NEW TOP DOG

I grinned for that camera. I batted my eyes. I did what any star should do.

Did they film me? No. Did they tell me how great I was? No? Did they ignore me? Yes.

The camera didn't even turn my way. All of the black-dressed strangers, including the ham lady, had their beady little eyes right on the bowl of Top Dog Tidbits.

The cameras rolled as a fluffy-haired creature gobbled every tasty morsel of the treats.

"Inspirational!" the ham lady said with a laugh.

"Perfect," the cameraman yelled.

"Sit, Sweetcakes," Fred said.

Sweetcakes did not want to sit. She wanted to get Tazz. But Fred held tight to the big bow, and the only thing Sweetcakes could do was whine.

"We'll call it the dog snacks so good, that even cats love them," said the ham lady.

That's when Tazz looked up from the Tidbits bowl, licked her lips, and winked. "Like I said, it's all a matter of timing," she purred at me, "and that is a Feline Fact!"